JUN 20 '00

E   Birchman, David
BIR   Francis
          Green horn blowing

E   Birchman, David
BIR   Francis
          Green horn blowing

The Blake Library

Martin County Library System
2351 S.E. Monterey Road
Stuart, FL 34996-3331

A Green Horn Blowing

A Green Horn Blowing

David F. Birchman

Illustrated by Thomas B. Allen

LOTHROP, LEE & SHEPARD BOOKS • MORROW

NEW YORK

I grew up during the Great Depression. Life was hard in those days, and a steady stream of worn men came through the trees onto my aunt Frita's berry farm, looking for jobs. She fed them all and put as many to work as she could. Most of them hung about for several weeks, then drifted off, but one old wanderer named John Cleveland Potts stayed on even after the harvest. My aunt Frita kept him busy cutting out dead raspberry vines, stringing wire, and repairing busted wooden flats.

He slept in the barn with the cats. It was an arrangement agreeable to everyone, because the barn was far from the house, and John Potts played the trumpet. Out there he was free to blow loud and long. The cats and I were his only audience.

Most times he'd play a piece whole and complete, but then he'd shock and dazzle me with a short powerful riff that froze the very hairs on my back. Oh, that trumpet of his was a wondrous thing. Its brass blurred like soft gold tallow when the light of a lantern danced along its shaft and bell. It was as if his fingers were holding a flame.

In bed at night I imagined holding John Potts's trumpet in my hands. I'd turn it over and over, admiring it in my mind's eye. The notion that I could possess a horn myself was almost beyond imagining.

On Saturdays John Potts and I would ride into town on the flatbed of my aunt Frita's truck. While Aunt Frita went about her errands, we'd window-shop. I liked the windows of the five-and-dime, and John Potts was partial to the haberdasher's window. But our favorite was the window of Hochstadt's Pawn Shop, where saxes, trombones, and trumpets hung tantalizingly over cramped trays filled with rings and pocket watches.

"Mr. Potts, can we go inside and look at the horns?" I asked one October day.

John Potts stared down at me. "I don't like going into pawn shops," he replied.

"But Mr. Potts," I said, "I've got a whole buck. My papa gave it to me when he left me with Aunt Frita."

"I'm sure your papa wouldn't want you wasting your money on a horn," said John Potts. "Besides, you can't buy a horn with a buck."

That afternoon Aunt Frita was taking longer than usual with her errands, so we two decided to walk back from town. I was still down in the mouth about not being able to buy a horn, but it felt fine to be ambling along in the presence of John Potts.

We had just walked past Evatz Cannery when John Potts spotted a vine poking out from the brush at the side of the road. "I do love squash," he exclaimed, "and if I'm not mistaken, this is a squash vine." He immediately left the road and began to track the vine back to its bud. I followed.

We descended a deep gully to the banks of Who Calls Creek, a ditch filled with black water and crawdads. There the vine crept over a rotted log and disappeared into some skunk cabbage.

"I wouldn't trail that vine any further, Mr. Potts," I hollered. "Not unless you want to fill your boots with water." He ignored me and gingerly pushed on. Suddenly he let out a loud whistle, clapped his hands, bent down, and plucked something from amidst the skunk cabbage.

"Do you know what this is, boy?" he asked, holding out a large green gourd unlike any I'd ever seen. The puckered end of the squash, which had been attached to the vine, was long, straight, and thin. Its middle section was swirled and crooked, while the other end flared out like the spout of a large watering can.

"That's no common squash," I said.

"No," allowed John Potts, "there's nothing common about it; this plant is a trombolia."

"What does it taste like?" I asked.

John Potts looked at me, shocked. "You don't eat a trombolia, boy— you *blow* a trombolia!" Then, holding the gourd with his right hand, he fit his left into its flared end, put the puckered end to his lips, and blew. Nothing. He wiped his lips and blew again. This time there came a faint sound like the bawling of a newborn calf. Then he placed it in my hands. "This trombolia will take some breaking in, but I have no doubt that a boy like you will soon have this green horn blowing."

It took me almost a week to coax my first sound out of that trombolia. Fortunately, John Potts was a patient man. "All it takes to play a horn," he said again and again, "is a whole lifetime." He taught me to form notes by tensing my lips against the puckered mouthpiece of the trombolia, and he taught me to hear a note before I played it. He taught me syncopation. He taught me how to mute and refine the tone of the trombolia by cupping my hand in its bell.

I have no idea how many hours that winter John Potts spent trying to make a horn player out of me. Time got lost in the playing. Then, one morning when John Potts was feeling under the weather, I decided to practice my playing off by myself. I put the trombolia under my arm and walked out across the woodlot to the middle of a snow-covered field where the wind was blowing bare and cold over the countryside. I had intended to practice a snip of music called "The Storyville Strut," but I found myself playing off the sound of the wind, casting loud pure notes into the far distance. For the first time, I felt that maybe I was a horn player.

Winter passed into spring and planting began. John Potts and I were put to work with the other men laying out the young berry plants. It was cold, wet work. Whenever there was a break, we crowded around a small, smoky fire, rubbing our hands and trying to feel the toes in our boots.

"John Potts, could you and the boy play us something?" the men would ask. "Could you play something to make us warm?" So John Potts and I would play with the cold, wet rain dripping down over the brims of our hats until my cheeks felt flushed red, as if brushed by a flame.

That summer I brought that trombolia with me each and every day into the berry fields. I played it in the morning riding on the damp boards of the flatbed, during the heat of the noon rest tucked into the shadow of the berry bushes, and at the end of the day while the pickers weighed their flats. I played it loud and I played it long.

Nothing but nothing meant as much to me as that green horn. Maybe that's why it took so long for me to admit that the trombolia was going to seed. I heard its tone become more brittle each time I put it to my lips. I saw brown spots appear on its skin, then slowly grow together into long dark streaks. Shortly before the end of the season, I discovered three dry cracks in the bell. Even then, I wouldn't believe it. I placed the puckered end to my lips and blew. The trombolia still made a sound, but that sound was nothing like a horn. It was low, weak, and breathless—a death rattle. Sadly, I carried it out to the far field and abandoned it in a clump of brown grass. Then I went to find John Potts.

He was sitting in the sun, cutting twine. He took in the news about the trombolia slowly while he continued his cutting. "I expected this would happen," he said at last. "A trombolia—however wondrous—is only a plant, and plants perish. The sad truth is that there are precious few things in this life that last forever."

I felt myself becoming angry. "If you knew this was going to happen, you should have told me, Mr. Potts. You had no business getting me worked up over something I couldn't hold on to."

"Maybe your trombolia is gone," he said, "but you made that green horn blow something sweet for a time. You're a horn player now and for life. And that's something you *can* hold on to."

I looked at my empty hands and then back at John Potts. My eyes welled up with tears, and I turned and ran toward the house.

The berry harvest was good to my aunt Frita that year. There was cash in the jar, and she began to get notions. She bought herself a new hat, then decided that I should go back to school full-time. School had been a hit-and-miss affair for me because Aunt Frita was always pulling me out when she needed an extra field hand. I should have been happy, but I wasn't—not entirely.

One late fall day I found myself drawn back to the field where I had left the trombolia. I approached it with a stick, to flip it over, I guess. Time, however, had had its way, and there wasn't much left to my horn but a dried husk. As I poked at it, the wind suddenly filled my ears with a loud pure note. I raised my empty hands to my lips, and I stood in that far field and blew a phantom horn in harmony with the wind.

It was only when I was entirely spent and ready to leave that I looked down at the husk one last time and spotted a fresh green vine trailing away. It cut across the field, winding and looping about like some crazy-minded serpent. I followed it to the edge of the field and under a barbwire fence, and it wasn't until I was halfway across the woodlot that I realized it was trailing straight into Aunt Frita's barn. My heart pounding, I threw open the doors and wildly scanned the gloom inside. Finally, I spotted the vine again. It went halfway across the dirt floor and stopped dead cold. I was profoundly disappointed. There was no trombolia.

I raised my eyes. On the far wall, directly in front of me, hung John Potts's trumpet. "Mr. Potts, Mr. Potts," I hollered. "Are you here?" But he was nowhere to be found, and his bedroll and satchel were gone.

I stood in the empty barn for a long time, holding John Potts's trumpet in my hands. Then I spoke as if he were there in front of me. "Mr. Potts, I don't know where you've gone, and I don't know if you'll ever be back for your horn. But I'll hold on to it for you, Mr. Potts. I'll hold on to it for always. That's a promise." Then I raised the horn to my lips and I played.

To Diane—my lovely wife
who has shown so many children where to find the magic of music.
DFB

To all those who continue to support the arts in education.
TBA

The illustrations in this book were done in pastel and colored pencil on Canson Mi-Teintes paper.
The display and text type is Goudy Old Style. Production supervision by Esilda Kerr.

Published by Lothrop, Lee & Shepard Books
an imprint of Morrow Junior Books
a division of William Morrow and Company, Inc.
1350 Avenue of the Americas, New York, New York 10019

Printed in Singapore

FIRST EDITION
1 2 3 4 5 6 7 8 9 10
Library of Congress Cataloging in Publication Data
Birchman, David Francis.
A green horn blowing / by David F. Birchman;
illustrated by Thomas B. Allen.
p. cm.
Summary: During the Depression, a farmhand teaches a young boy to play the horn
on a special gourd known as a trombolia, and the lessons teach him about life as well as music.
ISBN 0-688-12388-0 (trade) — ISBN 0-688-12389-9 (library)
[1. Farm life—Fiction. 2. United States—Civilization—1918–1945—Fiction.]
I. Allen, Thomas B. (Thomas Burt), ill.
II. Title. PZ7.B511877Gr 1995 [E]—dc20 93-34054 CIP AC